WILSON
GETS A WASH

Bath • New York • Singapore • Hong Kong • Cologne • Delhi • Melbourne

One day, the trainees were playing hide and seek in the park. Brewster closed his eyes while Koko and Wilson looked for places to hide.

"One, two, three..." counted Brewster, as Koko hid.
"Eighteen, nineteen, twenty," he called, as Wilson zipped around behind him.

"Ooooohh," Koko sighed, sad that he had found her so quickly. Brewster trundled on, looking for Wilson. Where was that chugger?

All the while, Wilson was
sneaking along behind his friend.
"I give up!" Brewster yelled.

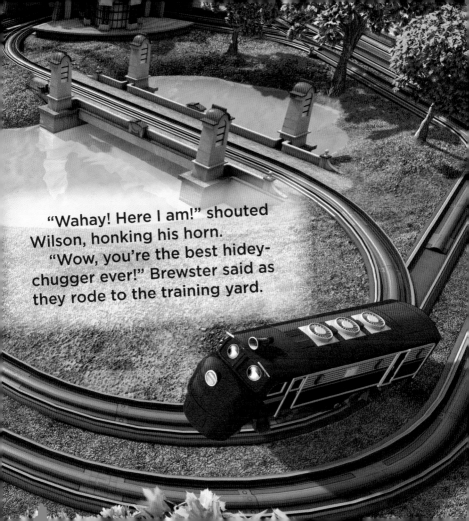

"Wahay! Here I am!" shouted Wilson, honking his horn.

"Wow, you're the best hidey-chugger ever!" Brewster said as they rode to the training yard.

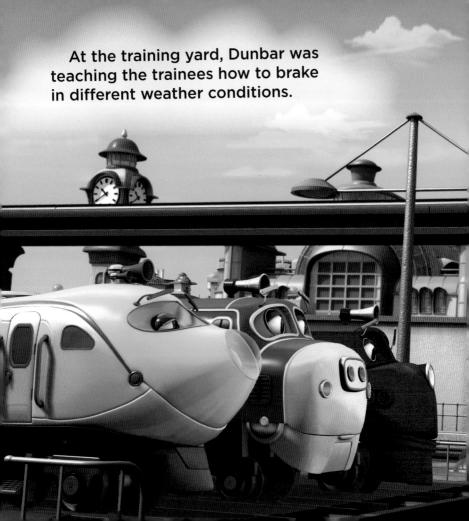

At the training yard, Dunbar was teaching the trainees how to brake in different weather conditions.

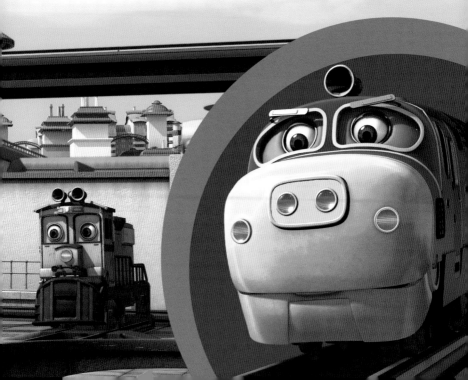

"Brilliant Brewster!" Dunbar called, when Brewster braked well on some dry leaves.

"Here I come!" cried Wilson, as he sped down the track. The leaves scattered everywhere, blowing up into his face so he couldn't see.

"Go slower!" Dunbar scolded, when Wilson skidded and banged into the bumpers.

SCREEEECH!

CRASH!

Next, Dunbar put mud on the rails.
Wilson zoomed into the big puddle
and splashed mud everywhere!

"WAHAY!

"Wahoo, Wahay! Woo-hoo!" he shouted as he went back and forth through the mud, getting really messy.

"All of you report to Lori for a clean up." said Dunbar.

WOO-HOO!"

When Koko, Brewster and Wilson arrived at the fuel yard, Lori showed them the new chuggwash. "It's like a great big shower for chuggers," she said.

Wilson wasn't so sure he wanted to be clean. "Ugh," he said to Peckham the dog, "Let's sneak away!"

Wilson rolled into the recycling yard and hid from Irving, who was sorting out the rubbish.

Suddenly, Irving tipped his load of rubbish straight into their hiding place. Being dirty was so much fun, Wilson decided to go and find more mucky things.

"Wahay!" called Wilson, as he sped into a mound of fresh grass in the park. "Messy, grassy, mess, mess, mess!" he sang.

"Whoa," he cried, slamming on the brakes just before a water sprinkler. "That was close. I nearly got clean!"

Meanwhile, at the depot, Koko and
Brewster looked shiny and clean.
"Where did Wilson get to?" asked Lori.

"Don't worry, we'll find him," said Koko.

Dirty Wilson saw Koko and Brewster searching for him and quickly hid from his friends.
"Mucky is more fun," he giggled.

Koko had a good idea to trap Wilson on the rails.

"Gotcha!" Koko cried, and they towed their naughty friend to the chuggwash.

"Noooo. Please don't make me," Wilson moaned as they entered the fuel yard.

"It's really fun, Wilson," Brewster said.

Spinning brushes tickled Wilson behind the gears.

"Oooo, actually, it feels quite nice!" he giggled. "I can't wait to get dirty again, then I can come back to the chuggwash."

Which picture of Wilson is the odd one out?

Can you join the dots to complete the picture? Then colour Wilson in!

Can you see where Wilson is hiding?

Answer: in the blue tunnel

Can you see which tunnel leads the trainees to the chuggwash?

Make your own Wilson!

1. Ask an adult to help you cut out the template carefully with safety scissors.

2. Fold the tabs inwards along the dotted lines.

3. Secure tabs with glue or sticky tape.

4. Add your stickers to each side.

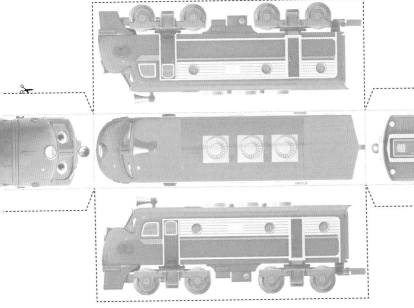

More chuggtastic books to collect!

Complete your Chuggington collection.
Tick them off as you collect!